Founder | CEO | Creative Director | Lovietta Simpkins
Editor in Chief | Leevette Simpkins
Literary & Creative Agent | Travis Walker
Author | Leevette Simpkins

This is a work of fiction. Not a portrayal or representation of any persons living or deceased. Not a portrayal of any organization or event. This novel is a product of the author's imagination and a work of fiction.

Envision & Wonder
First Edition Month & Year: June 2021
Publisher: Envision & Wonder
ISBN: 978-0-9961561-2-7

Blind Gambit

A Novel by Leevette Simpkins

Dedicated to Xavi and Bubba,
My Sun and My Moon.

Love Always, Leevette.

Prologue

"HELLPPPPP!!!! Somebody!!!! Please help!!!!!" Nina yelled in a terrified tone.

She looked back while running for her life. She didn't know how or why this was happening to her. In complete shock, rain ran down her red locs, trembling all the way down to her gray and white gym shoes. She had tears mixing in with the April showers.

In disbelief, she looked back again just to see him still running towards her. His eyes were bloodshot red. Completely in a trance of pure murderous rage. She looked forward and saw the lights on at the only coffee shop in town.

"HELP!!!!!" She banged on Sherry's brewery. The place where it all started. Where she met Dace Alex McCoy. She banged so hard on the glass window until she saw blood dripping down from her knuckles. Her heavy breathing was beginning to fog up the glass.

When she saw the barista's scared facial expression, she knew she was screwed.

Fuck this.

Nina knew all she could do now was fight her way out of whatever was coming. Clearly no one heard her cry for help. She began running again. Scanning through the area looking for something to possibly knock the shit out of him with. Her heart cracked more and more as the rain fell harder. So focused on getting away, she didn't notice how empty her surroundings were.

For some odd reason, the streets were clear. No traffic, no street lights, no innocent bystanders, just the sound of police sirens. She was running for the sake of saving her own life. She looked back and saw darkness. Then she stopped running to catch her breath.

I think I lost him.

Inhaling and exhaling with relief. She placed her right hand on her chest and felt her heart racing.

I need to calm down.

Nina knew her adrenaline would get the best of her if she didn't relax. Clearly she out ran him. After some shifty turns down alleys and janky side streets, she felt like she outsmarted him. She closed her eyes and her mind began to wander. Drawn into the night where he invited her over. Their first date at his condo.

He lived on the 4th floor of the Vine Condominium Complex. His door had the numbers 414 in a gold metallic color on it. She placed her finger on the numbers and took a deep breath.

What do I have to lose?

Her optimistic mindset always puts her into uncomfortable situations. But it was a good thing. She hated playing it safe. She balled her fist up to make her presence known, but he must've felt her state of being there because he opened his door before she could knock.

Her giggle was his weakness.

He gave her a smirk and said, "You look amazing."

Nina smiled, showing off her deep embedded dimples in her cheeks. "Thank you, you don't look too bad yourself, stud." She looked him up and down. She couldn't decide whether his casual all black attire matched with a bouquet of red roses or his alpha male aura was the reason why she was mesmerized by him.

"Come in love, don't be shy. I don't bite."

His smirk convinced her he was bullshitting. She walked into a dimmed lit atmosphere. Her eyes immediately zoned to the dinner table. Lit candles were the centerpiece. Garlic butter steak accompanied by a row of lightly fried shrimps and mashed potatoes laid beside it.

"Wow. Everything looks amazing." She looked around in awe as he pulled out her chair.

"Thank you handsome." She showed her appreciation by kissing his cheek as he traded off with the roses and pushed her chair in.

"For you, there's no thank you needed."

She smiled so hard he could barely see her hazel green eyes. He was drawn to them.

They were the reason he was determined to make her his. He blinked then said,

"So Nina..."

She was snatched back to reality when she felt his hand clenching her neck. Barely able to speak and breathe at the same time, she used the last bit of lively energy she had to say,

"WHY?"

I

"Get the fuck over here NOW!!"

He sat in the corner of his bedroom with his knees pressing up against his chest as he stared at his closed door. He could taste the blood dripping from his upper lip. It was busted from being punched by his inebriated father. This was the norm for him. Coming home to an angry unemployed father who blamed the world for his shortcomings.

"GET YOUR ASS OVER HERE!!!!"

All Dace could hear was glass being thrown and his mother fighting for her life. His mother always protected him. Unfortunately, she worked a later shift today which meant Dace had to walk home and prepare for the unimaginable.

He'd push him around every now and then but nothing compared to his father's fist connecting to his 9 year old jaw, knocking him to the ground.

When his mother opened the door to the house to see her son on the ground, she quickly pushed Markus to the floor.

"DACE GO TO YOUR ROOM!! HURRY!!"

His mother was terrified. She knew Markus had to be put in his place and didn't want her only son to see it.

Dace grew up knowing something was off with his dad. He noticed little things like the banging on the table if the food wasn't ready at the time he preferred. If he didn't like how it was cooked, he'd throw his plate at the wall. Or the grabbing of his mother's arm like she was a possession in public when they went places together. Dace never addressed any of it because he was a kid.

His mother made sure he was happy. Video games, books, musical instruments, whatever Dace wanted, he got. She protected him by distracting him through materialistic items. He wasn't stupid though, he knew.

"Markus you have to go!!" Tamantha yelled as she waved a bat towards his face.

"Bitch are you crazy!?" He responded while running towards her.

"When it comes to my child, absolutely. You put your hands on my flesh and blood. My reason for even having your dumb ass around and putting up with your shit." Fed up, she took a swing at him and missed.

He laughed at her and pushed her into the stove knocking over the gumbo she prepared prior to going to work.

"I will kill your ass in here!!" Markus grabbed her face and punched her in the nose. Before he could touch her again he heard,

"STOOOOPPPPPPP!!!!" Dace pointed a butcher knife at his dad hoping he'd protect his mother the way he felt he needed to.

"Dace no!! Go to your room!!" Tamantha yelled pleading to her son to leave the situation alone. She wouldn't forgive herself if he got hurt again.

She was forced to grow up and never really knew what it was like to protect anybody until she had her son. She was young when she met Markus. They both went to Caliburg High School. She had dreams of becoming a doctor and Markus had an aspiration to become a football player. When he tore his ACL he never was the same. The team didn't want him anymore.

He lost his athletic scholarship and fell into a deep depression. When Tamantha told her parents she was expecting a child, they were furious. They kicked her out and she ended up living with Markus and his mother.

She encouraged them to get married because she didn't believe in bastard kids. Markus' dad passed away when he was younger, so all he knew was his mother and trusted in her word. Tamantha was uneasy about it, but agreed to marry him because she didn't have anywhere else to go.

Unfortunately, his mother passed shortly after they graduated and Markus didn't take it well. He began drinking which caused him to lose the many jobs he got hired to work at.

Tamantha had no choice but to work and make sure Dace was straight. She started as a receptionist at a law firm but ended up becoming a paralegal when she was able to afford daycare. She didn't trust her husband to watch him.

Markus tended to take his frustrations out on her and she never wanted her son to go through it. She stayed because the house was his mother's and it was paid for. She had a roof over her and her son's head. Much better than being homeless with nowhere to go.

Tonight Tamantha realized she failed as a parent. She thought her son was distracted by all the things she bought him but he was observing everything. She was heartbroken that it came down to her staring at her child pointing a knife at his father while her face was aching from pain and leaking of bloody residue.

"Please baby, put the knife down." She pleaded with him as tears rolled down her face.

Dace ignored her as he stared at his father. "Let my mother go or I'll—"

Markus finished his son's sentence. "Stab me!? Come on nigga if you're gonna do it, make sure I'm not breathing afterwards." While laughing, he began to punch Tamantha in the face again.

Dace ran towards him and stabbed his father in the neck.

"NOOOOOO!!! What did you do!???" Tamantha pressed on. Markus' neck as the blood squirted uncontrollably through her fingers. "DACE!! Call 911!!!" She looked around the room for something to help stop the bleeding.

Markus was laying on top of her and his breathing was becoming faint. "Please!! Don't do this!!" She pleaded with Markus to fight to stay alive. At least until the paramedics could take over.

"DACE!! HELP ME!!" His mother pleaded and tears rolled down her face. This was the first vulnerable state he ever saw his mother in. She always had a strong persona around him but tonight... It was different.

Tamantha loved Markus from the moment they met on the first day of high school. She called it fate when they bumped into each other on their first day of being freshmen. Even when he spiraled out of control she still saw the good in him.

Markus stared into her eyes and took one last breath.

She cried so loud that she didn't even hear the paramedics knocking at the door. Dace closed his eyes and all he heard was the pain in his mother's voice.

He opened them and stared at himself in the mirror. He was doing it again. Zoning out to the day his life changed forever. The moment of weakness he witnessed with mother.

"I need to go see her." He said as he sipped on his glass of ice water on the sink.

My mother never recovered from that night. Hell I don't think I did either. She was the strongest person I knew. After that, man I don't know anymore.

He took his razor to his face to line up his facial hair. Dace has a caramel complexion. Short cut hair enough to show some curly texture. His freckles compliments his strong jaw line. His eyes are the color of a Jamaican ocean.

He's dark though. Very to himself, doesn't really like people bossing him around nor felt the need to be around them much.

That's why Dace owns a restaurant.

He pops in and out when he chooses and only deals with the money. His manager is his childhood friend Khalil who he told if he fucks up his money, he'll kill him. His favorite line is, "I killed my own father, don't think I won't hesitate to put your ass in a body bag too."

When he feels like stepping in the kitchen to show off his culinary skills, he cooks for the hell of it. Shows off in front of the chefs to make sure they stay on their toes.

He drives a black Jeep Wrangler with the windows tinted. A lot of his attire is black as well. He thinks black is the color of his soul. Usually when he leads with that on date, the women get weirded out and they tend to never go on a second one. He's poetic and likes to write when he's at home vibing out sipping on a Jack and Coke. He doesn't like inviting people over because of the energy they bring.

He looked at his matte black watch with gold trim and said, "Damn. I need some coffee."

He grabbed his keys and closed the door to his condo.

Dace got in his Jeep and drove to the only place he felt like matched his vibe. Sherry's Brewery is a staple in Icington. His mother used to take him there as a kid.

She would butter him up with a jumbo cinnamon roll and a hot chocolate while she barely ate because her stomach was sore from being punched in it.

"Hey Sherry, how are you?" Dace walked over and gave the owner a hug.

"Oh my gosh, I'm doing well!! I haven't seen you in a few days, what's been going on?"

Sherry is like another mother to me. Kept me on the straight and narrow when she knew my mother was having some rough days after my dad died.

"Well I'm trying to change up my restaurant. Bring in a few new things. Been kind of in my own world momma."

Yeah I call her that because my own mother gave me permission to.

"Okay sweetie there's nothing wrong with a little change. Don't get lost in that world of yours okay? I don't want to have to come find you." Sherry winked as she gave Dace his coffee.

"Thanks momma."

He turned around just to be stopped in his tracks. There stood a woman who he had never seen before. She looked around while carrying a pamphlet for newcomers to the city.

Wow. Who is she?

"I got this."

Nina loved to self motivate. Every morning she'd hit her alarm clock, sit up, and talk to herself. Not like a person who is mentally unstable, but you get my point.

It's my first day in Icington. I left my family to focus on my dreams of becoming a lawyer. I passed the bar, now the sky's the limit. I have my interview at 3 p.m so I need to make sure I'm on point.

Unlike Dace, Nina's upbringing was like a family sitcom. One of the good ones that everybody looked up to and wanted to be apart of. Her parents named her Nina Heaven Smith.

She was an only child, grew up in a suburban neighborhood, white picket fence, couple of dogs, the whole nine. Just because her home life was in tip top shape, that doesn't mean there wasn't challenges.

She grew up in a shell. Never really knowing if she could do anything on her own because her parents made sure they helped with everything. Until she decided to be a lawyer. She comes from a long line of doctors and well she didn't want to follow suit. Her dad is Dr. Reynolds Smith, world famous brain surgeon while her mother is Dr. Bena Jones-Smith, a world famous general surgeon. They met back in medical school.

They both bonded over their passions for changing the world one surgery at a time and both wanting one child after being established in their fields of study. They never thought about how their child would turn out. They always expected her to follow through with their legacy.

She didn't have many friends growing up because she stayed in the house with Nanny Joan. She basically was her best friend.

She knew about her hopes, dreams, and even her fears. When Nina graduated from high school, she knew she had to be honest with her parents. She didn't want to go to medical school and Nanny Joan encouraged her to talk to her parents about it.

Her mother cried while her dad gave her the silent treatment until she left to go to college. Joan was her emotional support throughout college and law school. She even helped her study to pass the bar.

Joan fell ill after Nina started to receive job offers at law firms. A lot of them were local but she convinced Nina to travel. Spread her wings and fly solo. Create her own legacy somewhere else.

After Joan passed away, she knew she needed to stay true to herself. She accepted the interview at Marmen & Stoaks Law Firm in Icington. A complete day's drive from her hometown in Marksburg. She figured if her parents ever came to their senses, she'd come back for holidays.

She tried to say goodbye to them, but neither one answered their phones or opened their door when she came by. She was sad about it but she knew she made the right decision to live for herself.

After a final attempt to reach out, she decided to write them a letter:

Hey Mom and Dad,

It's your daughter Nina. I know you might not read this anytime soon and that's okay. I just wanted to let you both know that I'm leaving town. I graduated out of college and passed the bar. I'll be starting my law career in Icington.

I know we haven't been in touch like we should, but in due time I hope you both can at least call me if you don't want to speak in person. I just wish you both understood me like Nanny Joan did.

I'm not saying you weren't exceptional parents, I love you both for everything you've done and taught me. The support for my dreams and goals was nonexistent.

I know you both don't feel bad about it but all my life I just wanted my parents to cheer me on for what I wanted to do with my life. Joan saw me for who I really was and I'm grateful she was there for me growing up. If it wasn't for her, I don't know where I'd be.

But anyways, I'm heading out. I've tried to contact you both and this my last resort. I wanted to make you both proud but I have to do that for myself.

I have to live for me and hopefully you both understand that at some point. My number hasn't changed since college but it's 314-788-9910. When I get where I'm going, I'll call again.

With love, Nina

With tears in her eyes, she pushed the letter underneath the door and got in her gray Chevy Cruze. She worked her ass off to buy her own vehicle.

Working full-time and going to school was a challenge, but she knew it would pay off.

She hopped out the shower, and began getting dressed. She looked around her pleasantly empty apartment and giggled. She knew she had the interview on lock.

She already was claiming her job before they even met her. After moisturizing her milk chocolate colored skin in Shea Butter, she put her white and black pinstripe button up on and accompanied it with a black pencil skirt.

She looked around her bedroom for her suitcase she packed her shoes in.

"There it is!!" Feeling relieved, she unzipped it and took out her black heels.

She looked in the mirror and placed her red locs in a bun leaving a few out in the front. She wasn't the type to wear makeup so she put on some nude colored lip gloss, diamond studded earrings with a matching necklace.

Something's missing.

She looked for her purse and grabbed her lucky watch and put it on.

I can't go anywhere without you Joan.

35

She called her watch by her nanny's name because it was a gift from her. It helped her achieve a lot of things throughout high school and college. After spraying her favorite cherry blossom perfume, her stomach started to growl.

Oh Jesus, I need to eat something.

She walked in her kitchen and looked in the fridge. Hoping the last tenant was kind enough to leave some eggs or something in there.

Shit.

The fridge was just as bare as every room in her two bedroom apartment. She figured she would possibly get a roommate or something if she got lonely or make the extra room into a home office.

She went to grab her purse again. She took out some pamphlets she picked up out of the gas station before driving to her apartment last night. She figured it could help her get around easier.

Sherry's brewery? Looks nice. It's been around for a couple decades. I could go for a stack of pancakes and bacon. Oh and coffee.

The reason why Sherry's had survived this long was because of what they specialized in. Coffee, desserts, breakfast, lunch, and dinner items. Whatever you had a taste for, it was definitely on the menu.

Nina grabbed her keys, briefcase, and her purse. She unlocked her phone and searched to see how far she was away from the brewery.

15 minutes isn't too bad. It's also 25 minutes away from the law firm.

She looked at the time on her phone. It was 10:00 am. She felt at ease because she didn't have to rush to eat and could enjoy the sites before her interview. She walked out the door and headed to the brewery.

Thank God there's a parking lot.

37

She parked her car then switched her shoes from her flats to her heels. She got her purse and walked into the brewery. The smell of maple syrup and coffee filled her nostrils.

She smiled.

There was a line to be seated so she patiently waited. She started to scroll on her phone but immediately got bored. Then she decided to look through the pamphlets. Little did she know when she looked back up, her life would change forever.

"Hello Mam. How many are in your party?" The waitress asked Nina curiously.

"Oh it's just-"

Before she could respond Dace quickly cut her off. "Two Terri." He smirked as he stared at Nina.

Who the fuck is this guy?

Terri grabbed two menus and started walking them to their table.

Dace immediately pulled out Nina's chair and she sat down.

She laughed and replied with, "Ummm, thank you."

"The pleasure's all mine sweetheart."

She smiled.

"Nice dimples." Dace smiled returning the gesture.

"I don't believe you introduced yourself Sir." Nina completely ignored his flirtatious vibes.

"Oh where are my manners. I'm Dace."

She looked puzzled. "Interesting name, I like it. I'm Nina."

"Well it's nice to meet you Miss Nina."

She looked down at the menu trying to distract herself. She needed something to take her eyes off the random guy who felt the need to have breakfast with her. She was intrigued by his effort to make himself known to her.

"I love the cinnamon rolls here." Dace decided to break the ice.

"Oh really? I'm guessing you eat here a lot."

"I do actually. I've been coming here since I was a kid. Nothing's changed and the whole staff knows me." Dace said confidently.

"That's nice. Hopefully the pancakes are as good as those cinnamon rolls." She began to chuckle.

"You won't be disappointed." Dace winked while signaling the waitress to come over and take their order.

"I'll have my usual Brenda. Pancakes for Miss Nina. The works please."

The works? What the hell...

"Got it D. Anything to drink mam?"

"Coffee please, 3 creams and 6 sugars. Oh and please extra butter on my pancakes."

"You got it mam." Brenda took their menus and walked towards the kitchen.

Nina took a sip of the complimentary glass of water and noticed Dace staring at her.

"What? Is there something on my face?"

Dace laughed then responded with, "No not at all. Your face is perfect."

His pickup lines are on point.

Nina started to laugh then immediately thanked him afterwards. "Thanks Mr. Dace."

"Tell me about yourself Nina."

He's nosey.

"Well…my name is Nina…"

Shit I told him that already. Get it together.

Dace nodded as he listened to her repeat herself. He knew she was drawn to him just like he was to her.

"I'm new to Icington. I'm trying to get a feel of some places here so I can get comfortable with being away from my family."

His right eyebrow raised and he posed a question.

"Oh you're here alone huh? How do you feel about that?"

Feeling a sigh of relief, she responded with, "Well so far it's been okay. I just got here last night. Soooo....yeah I guess what I'm saying is, I don't really know how to feel about it yet actually."

He smirked again and pondered up a response in his head.

This is gonna be very entertaining.

The waitress placed her coffee on the table and their food. Nina's eyes got really big. "WOW this food looks amazing."

Nina stared at her empty plate.

Damn I must've been really hungry. Pancakes, eggs, hash browns, bacon, sausage, grits with cheese and shrimp, and some toast.

"You have an appetite. I like that."

Dace knew she'd appreciate his cooking skills like no other woman in his past. His mother loved his cooking. He started making her food after his father died. Her appetite wasn't all that great, but she ate whatever he cooked. Good or not, she supported his craft.

Nina laughed and responded with saying, "Thank you." She looked at her watch and it said, "1:45 pm"

Dace noticed it so he stated, "in a rush huh? I'm that bad?" Taken back, Nina laughed and said, "oh no, I just have an interview I have to get to by three. It's about 25 minutes from here so I don't want to be late or get lost. I don't know my way around here."

Dace nodded in agreeance. "I can take you if you'd like."

He offered to help her so their encounter didn't have to end so quickly. He liked how they meshed together. A lot of women probably would've stopped him when he invited himself to their breakfast table. She didn't know him nor did he know her.

That's nice of him.

"Oh I'm okay. I have a car."

Looking a little defeated, Dace's response was, "well at least let me walk you to your car then. It's the least I can do."

Brenda brought the check to the table. Before Nina could lift her hand to grab it, Dace stopped her by saying, "What are you doing Miss?"

She chuckled and answered with, "oh, I thought I was going to pay for my food."

He shook his head no. "Whenever you're with me, I got us."

Alpha male, I wonder what he does for a living. Let me not be rude and thank him.

"Thank you."

He placed a one hundred dollar bill on the table and stood up. "Let's head out."

He walked her to her car and opened the door to the driver's seat. "You're such a gentleman."

He laughed and stated, "I was raised well."

She stared into his eyes and got lost. She didn't know what was more attractive. His demeanor or his model-like face. She thought his freckles were so cute. His muscular body type showed through his fitted black t-shirt. His Aztec tattoos glistened in the sunlight. She fought back trying to touch him. She just wanted to feel if the person standing in front of her was real.

He completely cut off her daydream by saying, "I want to see you again."

She stood in place contemplating whether she was happy or a little frightened by his statement. Nina never had a guy she was interested in on this level. She always had her head in the books, playing with the dogs, or spending time with Nanny Joan.

She had crushes in the past, but she never acted on them. They always went for the opposite of what she was. She didn't know how to respond to him. All she knew was maybe it would help her transition better if she hung out with someone that knew the city. "That would be nice." She smiled at him.

"Can I have your number? That way we can plan our next adventure?" Dace asked in high hopes she'd say yes.

She took a deep breath and answered with, "of course."

They exchanged numbers and she got in your car. He stared at her as he closed her door.

"Until next time Miss Nina." He smiled and winked at her.

She couldn't control herself.

"Bye."

She drove off thinking to herself,

Bye. What the fuck? I'm a loser. Did I say too little? Jesus, he's never going to contact me. I fucked it up.

Before she got to the first traffic light outside the brewery she felt her phone vibrate. She picked it up and it was a text message from a number that wasn't programmed in her phone. It said,

`(215)667-1411`

`Hey Miss Nina...`

The traffic light turned green, she smiled and drove off.

He put his phone in his pocket and walked back into the brewery.

"So who was that D?" Brenda asked as he walked toward the carry out counter.

Dace responded with, "my future wife."

They both laughed. Sherry walked out the kitchen and Dace handed her an envelope.

"Now you know how I feel about you giving me money sweetie."

Dace nodded and replied with, "I know but I have to make sure I properly thank you. You saved me."

She hugged him and kissed his cheek. "I got to go check on my restaurant. I'll check on you later Momma, love you."

She smiled and said, "I love you too." He got in his Jeep and drove off.

Dace looked at his phone and instantly started smiling.

It was a text from Nina.

Hey Mr. Dace

Before he could respond, his phone started to ring. It was his friend Khalil.

What the fuck does he want?

Dace answered the phone by saying, "Yo."

Khalil responded with, "Hey nigga where are you?"

"Aye are you at the restaurant?" Dace asked confusingly.

53

"Yeah, why?" Khalil sounding puzzled.

Dace shook his head.

This nigga is so unprofessional bro.

"You're not on the street. You gotta lead by example. Don't address me as a nigga when you're in my shit. You're gonna have mufuckas thinking they can talk to me any type of way." Dace said furiously.

"My bad. You're right." Khalil agreed.

Dace has been helping Khalil all their lives. They met when they were 10 years old. When Dace and his mother moved to an apartment complex, Khalil was his next door neighbor. They played in the courtyard, fought together, and even stole together. After Dace's father passed away his personality shifted. He wasn't the saint his mother raised him to be.

He acted like an angel around her but when she wasn't around, he was Satan. He use to be able to control his anger but when he became a teenager, it became more challenging to keep it under wraps. Khalil and Dace were walking home from high school when a bully nicknamed Chubbs crossed their path.

Khalil was scared of him because of the rumors about him nearly killing a guy because he didn't agree to do his homework.

"You're in our way nigga." Dace said annoyingly.

Breathing heavily, Chubbs responded with, "No I'm not bitch. Khalil knows why I'm here."

Before Khalil could respond, Dace replied with, "who the fuck are you talking to?"

Chubbs laughed and said, "You bitch. Run my money Kha—"

Before he could finish his statement, Dace punched him in the nose. Before Chubbs could catch himself, Dace punched him in his nose again knocking him to the ground. All Dace saw was red.

"Yo D STOOPPPP!!" Khalil yelled in a worried tone.

"Nah fuck that!!" Dace continued to punch Chubbs while blood started to splatter on his shirt.

Out of nowhere, a woman yelled "HEY!!! Cut it out!!"

She pulled Dace off of Chubbs and Khalil ran away.

"Dace!? What the hell are you doing!??" It was Sherry from the brewery. She recognized him because his mother always brought him there every Saturday and Sunday.

"This nigga called me a bitch." Dace said while catching his breath.

Sherry shook her head. "Get in this restaurant. NOW." She stared at both the boys and they both walked in her establishment.

"Here you go baby." She handed Chubbs a ziplock full of ice chips.

Chubbs wiped his nose with some napkins then put the ice chips on his face. "Thanks lady."

"Dace get over here." She stared him down as he walked over with his fists still clenched.

"So you're gonna punch me now? Put them fists down boy before I slap you."

Dace listened.

"Apologize. Both of you. You're too young to be fighting out in the street like some riff raff. Dace you know good and well your momma raised you better than that. And as for you, what's your name sweetie?"

"Chubbs." He sniffled.

She stared at him.

"Okay It's Gregory."

"Gregory how old are you?"

He responded with "17."

"Dace why the hell are you fighting a 17 year old? You're barely a freshman in high school."

"Look Sherry he disrespected me."

"How? Calling you something you know you're not?"

Dace looked down at the floor.

"Listen. There are much more important things to worry about besides calling each other obscenities. Let me catch y'all fighting again and Imma beat both of your asses myself. Do I make myself clear?"

"Yes." Gregory and Dace said in unison.

Gregory got up and headed for the door.

Dace started to follow him but Sherry pulled him back. "I'm calling your mother." Dace looked at her worried.

"No mam you can't do that." Dace knew if she found out about what happened she'd flip her lid. She had just got over him being suspended for fighting, now to find out he almost knocked somebody out? Yeah he had to smooth things over with Sherry.

"Look. I can't disappoint her anymore than I have already. Please don't call my mother." Dace pleaded with Sherry. He even dropped a tear.

"I'm worried about you Dace. Your mother and I talk about you all the time. She thinks you're going down the wrong path."

He stared at the floor.

"Look at me. We are not gonna lose you to no foolishness. I lost my son 8 years ago to the streets. I refuse to let another one I hold dear to my heart slip away. Do you hear me?" She put her hand on his chin so he could focus on what she was saying.

He looked her in her eyes and said, "yes mam."

She nodded. "Your mother told me you know how to cook."

"Yes mam I cook for her all the time. I love it." Dace smiled.

"Okay let's make a deal. I'll let you help me out around here, clean up, cook, and whatnot IF you maintain good grades and stop the fighting. Oh and I also won't call your mother about today." Sherry smirked.

Dace's face lit up. "Yes mam that would be awesome."

"I'll also pay you, that way you'll have some cash in your pocket. Let's start you off on weekends. I'll let your mom know."

Dace smiled and responded with, "Thank you mam. But can Khalil help out too? Chubbs, I mean Gregory brought up how he owes him money. I'm pretty sure it'll help him pay the guy back."

Sherry sighed and said, "Okay D. That's fine. Let him know both of you start Saturday around 12 pm. I could use the extra hands for our lunch hours."

She handed him some to go containers filled with food to take home. Sherry said, "just heat it up for dinner."

"Thanks mam." Dace walked out the brewery and headed home. He saw Khalil sitting on the stoop outside the apartment complex.

"I'm sorry D, I got scared." Khalil said that as Dace handed him a container of food.

61

"What was that fat nigga talking about?" Dace questioned him.

"Nah, he wanted to take my lunch the day you weren't at school. I didn't give it to him, so he said I gotta pay for his lunch everyday until he feels like stopping me." Khalil responded while eating a french fry.

Dace shook his head. "Nigga. Why didn't you just give him your lunch bro?"

"Because I was hungry. You know my mom is barely home and she don't cook." Khalil took a bite of the cheeseburger.

"Look. I don't know how much money you owe dude, but I can't get into any more fights. My momma is still on edge from the last one. Talking about sending me away and shit."

Khalil looked at him shocked. "Damn bro, it's that serious?"

"Hell yeah." Dace shook his head. "We'll be working for Sherry until further notice. Pay his ass when she gives us our money for helping her out. Talk to dude and work something out because I'm not gonna fight dude every time I see him. You know I'll kill his ass."

Khalil nodded in agreeance.

Ever since that day, Dace made sure Khalil was on the straight and narrow because if he fucked up that meant he had to result back to his old ways. Dace wanted to move forward not backwards.

Sherry helped Dace improve his culinary skills while showing both of them how to run a successful business because Khalil needed a life plan and Dace said he wanted to open his own restaurant one day.

Dace saved every penny she gave him until he finally had enough to get his own restaurant. He didn't trust anybody but his best friend with his money and keeping his restaurant intact so he made him the manager. He still had to keep him on his toes and smack him up a little bit, but he knew Khalil wouldn't fuck him over.

"I'm pulling up. Meet me outside." Dace parked in his designated parking spot.

"Iight bro." Khalil hung up.

Dace got out his Jeep, texted Nina, and looked up at his restaurant's sign. It read "Tammy's."

He smirked, raised his eyebrow and said, "Showtime baby."

Dace:

You should let me cook for you.

Nina:

Oh really?

Dace:

Yeah. I kinda know how to cook and I'm pretty sure you didn't go grocery shopping yet.

Sigh...well he's right.

Nina:

I'll indulge.

Dace smiled as he saw her response.

Oh she just doesn't know what she's getting herself into.

Dace:

So it's a date then huh?

Nina:

I guess so lol

Dace:

How's 8:00 pm?

Nina:

Perfect. That gives me some time to change.

Dace:

18000 E. Jayway Ave

Vine Condominium Complex

4th Floor, room 414

Nina:

Perfect. I'll see you at 8.

Dace:

Good luck on your interview beautiful.

She smiled. Before she could reply, the receptionist called her name.

"Nina Smith, they're ready for you."

Nina got up and said, "Thank you."

Nina walked into the conference room and shook hands with the founders of the law firm.

"Good afternoon Miss Nina, I'm Mr. Marmen and this is Mr. Stoaks"

Nina smiled and responded with, "It's nice to meet both of you. Thank you for this opportunity."

They both nodded.

Mr. Stoaks started the interview by saying, "so tell us a little bit about yourself. We know you have a degree in law, passed at the top of your class, as well as passed the bar. Why us?"

Nina took a deep breath and responded with, "Well I did a lot of research on this particular law firm and I liked what I found. Your law firm takes on challenging cases. You guys win a huge chunk of them, there's no controversy behind any of your lawyers, plus your law firm believes in taking pro bono cases. Not to mention it's very interactive with the community. I want a challenge and want to feel like I belong somewhere. Your law firm makes your lawyers feel like they are family. I need that in my life. I feel like with my quick thinking and strategic mindset, I will be an asset to your firm."

Mr. Stoaks and Mr. Marmen looked at each other and nodded.

Mr. Marmen extended his hand out and said, "Enjoy your weekend. We'll see you Monday morning at 8 am."

Nina shook his hand and responded with, "thank you so much!! I can't wait."

They all smiled.

Mr. Stoaks said, "see our receptionist Jenny for your parking pass. Make sure you keep it in your car every day you work."

Nina nodded then they all walked out the conference room. She was so excited that she got the job, she attempted to call her mother.

She didn't answer.

She called her father, he didn't answer either.

She sighed then texted Dace.

Nina:

I got the job!!

Dace:

That's wonderful Nina, congratulations sweetheart.

Nina smiled uncontrollably. Then quickly responded.

Nina:

Thank you so much.

Dace:

No need to thank me. I knew you had the job the moment you told me you had an interview. How could they say no?

Nina:

Well I'm going to head home to freshen up then meet up with you. Should I bring anything?

Dace:

Just your pretty ass face and your powerful presence.

Nina giggled and got in her car.

Nina:

Lol okay. I'll see you tonight.

Dace:

Later.

Shit. I don't know what I'm going to wear.

She drove back to her apartment and immediately started throwing clothes everywhere. She was overthinking everything. Dresses everywhere, shirts, and ripped jeans were on the floor next to her inflatable mattress.

Okay Nina, breathe. It's not that deep. I'll just wear something casual.

To calm herself down, she took a shower. She closed her eyes as the hot water fell on her face then her body. She zoned out.

After her shower, she oiled her body, and began to get dressed. She decided to wear her red v-neck shirt with gold splattered paint on it along with her black ripped jeans. She picked out a black biker jacket with gold buckles plus some black and gold boots to bring her outfit to life. She decided to let her locs hang loosely with a few tucked behind her ear. She put her red lipstick on and sprayed her perfume on right after. She put her gold hoops on while a gold diamond pendant laid on her chest.

Damn Nina.

She laughed then walked out the door.

Khalil walked out of Tammy's and gave Dace a handshake dab.

Dace nodded and said, "what's up nigga, how's my sales?" Khalil smiled and responded with, "they're good. We made a 75% sales increase in the past week. People are loving that new lobster dish."

Dace smiled and said, "good, that's what I like to hear. How's my speed of service?"

Khalil coughed and said, "The new nigga Jake is a bit slow with getting the orders out. He messed up a few tables last week. I talked to him and told him he needed to get his shit together."

Dace shook his head in disappointment. "He fucking up my money. Cut his ass."

Khalil's eyes got big and he stated, "bro calm down, he's young I can mold him into somebody great. Be patient damn."

Dace stared at him in his eyes and said, "I'm giving him one more day. I'll be back tomorrow to watch him. If I don't like what I see, I'm taking him off my payroll. That nigga fucking up my business. The more he fuck up, the less people he's gonna serve which means my business will go up in flames. That's unacceptable. I'm not losing my shit for anybody. I won't hesitate to pull his tickets, see how much he made and calculate how much more he could've made and take that shit from your check. Don't fuck with me."

Khalil nodded and said, "Damn nigga, it's like that?"

Dace blinked and said, "I got places to be and people to see. Pull my sales report, payroll, the whole nine. I'll be back tomorrow to pick it up and make sure you count my meat right for inventory nigga."

Khalil laughed, "I got you bro."

They dabbed again, and Dace headed back to his condo.

I'm thinking steak, shrimp, and potatoes.

He started seasoning the steak and shrimp. He knew she'd like his food but he needed more to impress her. He went to his rose bush on his balcony and cut off a dozen roses.

He loved candles so he set some up on his dining room table. He checked the steaks and shrimp. They were cooking perfectly so he started to make his mashed potatoes from scratch.

After completing the dinner, he hopped in the shower and got dressed. He decided since he's hosting, he'd dressed the part.

Black button up with gold cuff links, pitch black jeans, with a pair of all black casual shoes to match. He put on a gold chain and put on a gold watch to match it. His cologne had an earthy scent that smelled like rosewood. It definitely complimented his masculinity.

He put a little moisturizer in his hair to bring out his curls, he added beard oil to his facial hair, and smiled at himself in the mirror.

He took a look around his condo. He wanted to make sure everything looked amazing for Nina. Even though it wasn't their first time meeting each other, he wanted his space to feel welcoming. He didn't really invite people over so in his mind he knew she was special.

He looked at his metal clock on the wall. It read 7:30 pm.

She should be arriving soon.

He checked the food and everything tasted exceptionally delicious. He didn't want to add his garlic butter to the steaks until the last minute. He knew presentation is key. He took out his black plates and set them on his counter in the kitchen. He placed everything on the plates and set them on his dining room table. After he did that, he heard footsteps.

She's here.

He picked up the bouquet of roses and went to open the door. Completely surprised at what he saw, he said, "you look amazing."

Nina smiled and replied with, "thank you, you don't look too bad yourself, stud."

They both smiled at each other then he invited her in. She looked around and immediately loved what she saw. She knew he had put a lot of thought into their date because of how the presentation looked.

"Let me show you around real quick." Dace held out his hand for her to grab. She grabbed his hand and he gave her a tour.

Damn he's really doing good for himself. I hope he's not a drug dealer.

"Let me put your jacket in my closet." Dace grabbed her jacket then led the way to his dining room table. He pulled her chair out and gave her the bouquet of roses. She gave him a slight peck on his cheek then admired the food on the table.

"Wow everything looks amazing." Nina said surprised.

"I try." Dace said, trying not to sound too cocky.

They started to eat and Nina closed her eyes. She let her steak marinate in her mouth and tasted all the seasonings plus the garlic butter. The steak was cooked perfectly and she felt like she was in heaven.

"Oh my God. This is so good." She fought back tears of happiness and enjoyment.

"I'm glad you like it." Dace smiled.

"So tell me about yourself." Nina said curiously.

"Hmmm let's see, I'm Dace, a grown ass man, I own a restaurant, drive a Jeep, owned this condo for about five years, father's dead, mom is kinda out of it now, only child, have one best friend, and he's the manager of my restaurant. Oh and my favorite color is black because it defines my soul."

Nina's eyes got big then she laughed. "Wow, you're pretty interesting."

Taken back, he asked, "I hope that's a good thing?"

Nina stated while feeding herself some mashed potatoes, "oh it is. So you own your own restaurant? Tell me about it."

Dace smiled and replied with, "I named my restaurant after my mother, it's called Tammy's. It specializes in high end seafood, top notch steak dishes, and cinnamon inspired desserts. All her favorite foods. I opened up after I got my business degree."

Nina nodded.

Dace proceeded to say, "Sherry from the brewery took me in as a teenager, showed me the ropes, and helped me enhance my cooking skills. I knew if I didn't know my shit, how could I expect my employees to? So I became a chef as well. I teach them every now and then about a new dish I want to try out and also stop in and taste their dishes to make sure they're serving the best."

"That's amazing you seem very determined to succeed." Nina said confidently.

Dace nodded in agreeance then said, "I already know your name, tell me about why you're here."

Nina looked up from her plate and responded with, "My passion is helping people. I moved out here to pursue that."

Dace looked surprised.

Nina laughed and asked, "what? I don't look like somebody that could be interested in that?"

He smirked and replied with, "actually you do. I believe I owe you a bottle of wine to congratulate you for getting your dream job."

He got up to go over to his fridge. He asked, "red or white?"

She replied with, "surprise me."

He picked out his favorite red wine, smirked, then brought it to the table.

"This one is my favorite. Jeana Dior, 1991." He popped the cork and poured some into their glasses.

Nina looked amazed then said, "wow how did you get that? They've been sold out everywhere for months."

He smiled and said, "I got connections."

They both laughed. She got up and walked towards his windows in his living room. They showed the city's skyline.

"This view is beautiful." Nina said in awe.

Dace got up and walked towards her saying, "just like you."

He placed his hand on her cheek and leaned in for a kiss. Nina decided to reciprocate the gesture. In that moment, they both got lost in each other. Their kiss was so passionate, it felt like they had known each other forever. Their connection in that moment convinced them both that they needed to explore more.

Dace pulled back.

"What's wrong?" Nina asked puzzled.

"I'm a gentleman before anything, I'm sorry. I just couldn't help myself." Dace began walking back towards the dining room table. He picked up the dishes and placed them in the sink.

Nina walked towards him. She turned him around and said, "it's okay."

Their eyes locked into each other. When she smiled, her deep rooted dimples revealed themselves and he lost it. He picked her up and placed her on the kitchen counter. He began to kiss her neck and ripped her shirt off in the process. She unbuttoned his shirt and ran her fingers over his six pack.

He then grabbed her neck, kissed her lips, and told her, "lay down."

He wanted to please her. He knew if he did, it would be hard for her to let him go.

He kissed every inch of her body and then began tasting her forbidden fruit. She grabbed his curls as he continued to eat what he thought of as his dessert. After coming up for air, he licked his lips then kissed her.

He placed his hands in her hair, while slowly working them down to her face. They both locked eyes again and kissed again.

Dace stared at her and said, "spend the night."

Nina smiled and replied with, "okay."

He picked her up, took her to the bedroom, and laid her down on the bed. "Wait what about the dishes?" Nina asked curiously.

Dace responded with three simple words, "fuck them dishes.

VII

The ray of sunshine broke through his vertical black blinds. It was Dace's alarm clock. He stared at Nina laying on his chest.

Damn she's beautiful.

He caressed her face with his hand. He lifted her head carefully to free his body. He got up and walked towards his kitchen. He immediately shook his head and smirked.

Yeah, shit definitely got real last night.

He started to put the dishes in the dishwasher. He then began to look at his clock. It was 9:00 am. He took out the ingredients to make French toast, eggs, and bacon. As he started to cook, he began to daydream about the first day he made French toast for his mother.

It was raining so hard it made a banging noise on the window pane.

"Ma did you eat today?" Dace asked his mom curiously after getting off the school bus and walking in the door to their apartment. In a daze, she ignored him. He shook his head as he tied up the overflowing garbage in the trash bag.

He washed his hands and looked on top of their refrigerator and saw the bread. He couldn't remember the last time his mom went out to the grocery store so he opened up the spice cabinet. He saw cinnamon and sugar.

French toast.

That was one of the first things he learned how to properly make at Sherry's brewery. He scrambled some eggs to go with it then made his mom's plate.

"Here you go Ma."

She grabbed the plate and continued to stare out the window. She then proceeded to ask, "Where's Markus plate honey?"

Dace stood there silent. After catching his breath, he responded with, "Ma he's gone."

Looking surprised, she said, "GONE!? Where is he?"

Dace immediately snapped back to reality when his phone vibrated on the counter. It was Khalil. Dace picked up the phone and said, "Grand rising homie."

Khalil responded with, "Yo good morning nigga. What's good."

Dace shook his head then replied with, "Nigga you called me. The restaurant don't open until 11 so what's up."

Khalil began to chuckle then stated, "Aw yea. Shit Barken late with his payment. He didn't come to the restaurant yesterday to drop it off. No call or nothing."

"This the second time bro. What the fuck are you doing? Now I gotta go break this nigga's legs." Dace started to put the French toast and sides on the plates.

"Nahhh Imma handle it. You don't need to get tied up in it. You are too important for that shit." Khalil said with reassurance.

"You got 30 minutes to handle it. Meet me at the spot in 45." Dace hung up the phone before he could respond.

I always gotta get my hands dirty in this bullshit. Nigga can't keep shit in order. Always letting shit slide.

He walked into his room, fixed his face with a fake smile and said, "good morning beautiful."

Nina's eyes opened to a work of art standing in front of her with a plate of deliciousness. He stood there, chiseled melanin physique wrapped in a black towel. She smiled and responded with, "all this is for me?"

He nodded then kissed her on her forehead. He looked at his clock and knew he needed to meet up with Khalil soon. He stated, "I have some business I have to tend to. My condo is yours. Make yourself comfortable, I'll bring you some clothes back, then we can go out and explore the city."

She bit her French toast, then said, "What about your plate? Are you going to eat before you go?"

He turned around after getting a white t-shirt out his closet that read, "Black King" then responded with, "I ate a little while I was cooking. I'll be okay love. Just enjoy yours."

He laid out his clothes on the bed then hopped in the shower. He rubbed his body with his lotion, got dressed then headed out the door. He began to dial Khalil's number. It rung twice then went to voicemail.

What the fuck!?

He tried again but no luck. He drove to Barken's laundromat. He saw Khalil's white Range Rover parked. The door to the laundromat was cropped open with a brick. Dace opened his glove compartment in his car and picked up his gun. He placed it inside his waistband then covered it up with his shirt.

Here I go picking up the fuckin pieces.

He got out of his car and proceeded to walk in the door. All he heard was Khalil yelling.

"I told you last time not to pull this shit again! What the fuck is your problem!?" He then began to punch the man until his face was covered in blood. Dace ran towards Khalil and pulled him off of the guy.

Dace then yelled, "This isn't how we do business anymore more nigga!"

Khalil stared at Dace out of breath and responded with, "I gave this dude a warning last time. I had to send a message."

Barken laid there on the ground lifeless as the washing machines continued to run.

Look at this fuckin mess.

Dace walked toward the counter and grabbed a towel. He tossed it over to Barkin then proceeded to ask, "Do you have my money?"

Barkin wiped his face got up and walked to his safe. He grabbed two bags out the safe and handed it to Dace.

"Do I need to count this shit?" Dace stared him in his eyes.

"No it's all there. I promise." Barkin said with a shaky tone.

Khalil looked at Barken and said, "this is your last payment. Congrats nigga."

Dace shook his head and said, "don't even think about going to the police either. I know where you stay."

Khalil proceeded to reach for his gun. Dace stopped him by saying, "Nah nigga. Not today. Let's go."

As they proceeded to walk out, Dace heard a gun being cocked behind him. He turned around and saw Barken about to pull the trigger on Khalil. He quickly went for his glock and emptied his clip on Barken.

Khalil turned around and saw Barken drop to the floor. "What the hell just happened!??"

Dace put his gun back in his waistband and covered it up with his shirt. "That nigga was trying to kill you. I had to lay his ass out."

Dace took out his phone and proceeded to dial a number.

"Yea, come to the laundromat and clean this shit up." Dace said while looking down at his shirt. He saw blood splatter on it. He shook his head and took the shirt off. He then looked at Khalil and said, "Let's go nigga."

Dace put the "closed" sign on the door and shut it.

I need a new shirt.

"Go to my restaurant and get shit in order. I'll be there to watch that slow nigga." Dace dabbed Khalil and drove off.

Khalil nodded then stated, "It's gonna be a long day."

97

Jesus this place is so big.

Nina looked around Dace's condo while putting her empty dishes in the sink. She proceeded to wash them.

He really knows how to cook.

As she proceeded to clean her dirty dishes, she heard the door open. Dace walked through wearing a black shirt, diamond Cuban link chain, black jeans, and black shoes to match. She looked at him puzzled then asked, "wait didn't you wear a white shirt when you left?"

Shit she remembered.

"Yea but I wasted some coffee on it. Had to change." Dace handed her a bag from Lenny's Clothing Outlet.

"Go get dressed, I wanna show you my restaurant." Dace took over washing the dirty dishes and gave her a kiss on her cheek.

She smiled and responded with, "Okay."

Nina then walked to the bathroom and took a shower. She stood in the shower as the water flowed through her locs. Her eyes closed just reminiscing about her last summer with Joan. The summer she knew she had to become more independent and move forward with her own dreams. She smiled because she knew she was going to love her job as a lawyer. She had finally proved to herself that walking out on faith paid off. She cut the shower off and dried her body on his black towel.

He really loves black.

She walked out the bathroom and saw her clothes laid out. She saw roses laying right next to them. She smiled and proceeded to get ready. She put her cheetah print v-neck shirt on then her ripped dark washed jeans.

She saw a box by his dresser with a note on it. It simply said, "open me," she opened it to see some red pump heels. She smiled and put them on.

Perfect fit.

She let her hair just lay in its natural form so it could air dry. Putting a couple of locs behind her ears so they didn't hide her face. Nina looked for her lipgloss in her purse. Then proceeded to put her strawberry scented gloss on and walked out his room.

"I'm ready." Nina stood in front of him as the sun shined glistened on her perfect skin.

Dace smiled and said, "let's head out." When he opened the door it was a cop standing in front of him.

His eyes widened and then Dace proceeded to say, "Is there a problem officer?"

The cop stared at him then responded with, "Dace don't play with me."

Nina stood there in shock. She didn't know what was going on. She then asked, "Is everything okay Dace?"

Dace nodded then told her, "Yea just go sit on the couch. I gotta talk to this cop." He closed the door behind him and said to the cop, "let's take a walk."

"What's up?" Dace asked.

"Gunshots were heard and reported coming from Barken's laundromat earlier. No body was found but his wife is worried. She hasn't heard from him and is considering putting a missing person's report in. Do you know anything about him going missing?" The cop said while walking down the hallway of the condominium.

"Nah man. I been here." Dace nodded.

The cop laughed then responded with, "oh yea? So why were you spotted leaving the scene?" He showed him pictures of his car being seen on a traffic camera pulling out of the parking lot.

Fuck.

"Look bro, I don't know what you're talking about. I'm not the only nigga with a jeep in this town. Fuck off."

The cop nodded then said, "okay Dace. I'll see you again. This was a courtesy visit."

The cop then walked to the elevator and disappeared after walking inside it.

What the fuck!?

Dace shook his head then proceeded to go get Nina.

"Let's go." He peeked in his condo and saw she was sitting on the couch.

They both got in his jeep and drove to Tammy's.

"This is it. My prized possession. My everything." Dace smiled while opening her door.

Nina looked around and said, "this place looks amazing."

"Thank you beautiful." Dace kissed her on the forehead then proceeded to walk into his restaurant. Business was booming. All the tables were filled with customers. All the waiters and waitresses were doing their jobs effortlessly.

The cooks were receiving orders back to back but you couldn't notice because they were completing orders as quick as they were receiving them. Sweat was dripping from all of their faces as soon as they saw Dace. They all nodded then proceeded to complete orders. Dace walked towards the restaurant greeter after making his rounds then said, "Where's Khalil?"

"He's in his office." The greeter said while crossing out a name on his waitlist. He then stated on the microphone, "Jones party of 8!! Come this way please."

"Iight thanks Brody. Good job." Dace dabbed him then turned to Nina. "Go get something to drink at the bar. Tell em it's on me."

Dace walked to Khalil's office and said, "Knock knock."

Khalil looked up after looking at his sales intake for the hour. He responded with, "Yo." Dace closed his door and said, "Nigga we got a problem. A cop came to my crib. We gotta figure out what we're gonna do about this shit. It ain't going away. Mufuckas saw my jeep leaving the laundromat."

Khalil stood up and said, "what the fuck!?? Imma take care of it."

Dace looking puzzled said, "How bro?"

"That nigga Chubbs gonna take the fall. He owes us one anyway." Khalil walks toward the safe and grabs the deposit bag.

They both walk out the back exit to his jeep. Dace takes two bags of money out and hands it to Khalil.

"The mufucka got rid of the dead body, but his wife is still here bro. She's thinking about filing a missing person's report. She gotta get dealt with." Dace took out a cigar and proceeded to smoke it while Khalil put the money in the deposit bag.

"Chubbs wouldn't be alive if it wasn't for you D. He owes you. It's time to check in on that favor." Khalil zipped the bag closed.

Dace puffed smoke out his nostrils then dialed Chubbs number.

"Yo." Chubbs said while driving from a factory site two hours out of town.

"Aye Nigga meet me at the spot tonight." Dace dabbed Khalil then walked back in the restaurant.

"Iight D." Chubbs hung up the phone.

Dace thought about every possible outcome to the situation. He knew for sure he wasn't going back to jail. He went to jail doing a 5 year bid in Icington Correctional facility. He beat a guy to the point he went blind. Dace was on his way home from Sherry's Brewery when he saw Chubbs being held up in the alley a couple of blocks away from his condominium.

Granted Chubbs and Dace weren't on the best of terms but he saw it as, nobody fucks with his people. They were from the same hood, grew up on the same streets. They had the one altercation but respected each other afterwards.

He protected Chubbs by beating him up. Unfortunately the cops caught him before he could get away. He did his bid and only contacted Khalil, Sherry, and his mother. 5 years later, he ran into Chubbs at the gas station. He thanked Dace for what he did and told him whatever he needed no strings attached he'd do it.

Dace walked back into the restaurant and saw Nina at the bar. She was drinking a vodka tonic. He smiled and accompanied her. "Hey beautiful." He said while running his fingers through her hair.

About damn time he came back.

"Hey." Nina responded while sipping on her drink.

"So what do you think about my restaurant?" Dace asked confidently while looking around for Jake. He wanted to see how slow he really was.

"It's a beautiful establishment. It looks really nice and everything is running swiftly." Nina took a napkin off the counter and wiped her hands with it.

"So what else do you wanna do today?" Dace asked curiously.

In deep thought, Nina responded with, "your safe place."

Dace laughed and then said, "huh?"

107

Nina shook her head and said, "the place you go to to clear your head. It may help me out one day if I fall on rough times."

He nodded, took out a hundred dollar bill, placed it on the counter and said, "Okay. I got you. Let's roll."

Khalil walked over to Dace before they walked out the door. "What did you think about Jake and who is this?"

Dace shook his head and responded with, "My bad, where are my manners? This is Nina."

Khalil shook his hand and said, "I see you nigga."Nina laughed and Dace continued the conversation by saying, "Jake is too slow. Cut em."

Khalil shook his head and stated, "Iight."

"Send me the inventory sheets so I can put the shipment order in. We're leaving." Dace grabbed Nina's hand and guided her out the door.

He opened her door to his jeep then proceeded to drive. Nina said to herself, *this is going to be interesting.*

"Wake up my love. We made it." Dace said as he rubbed her cheek.

She sat up and responded with, "where are we?"

Dace laughed then replied with, "Icington Harbor. Our beach. I find myself coming here a lot just sitting at the pier pondering about life. My mother use to take me here when she'd run from Markus. He'd eventually find us though."

Nina asked curiously, "who's Markus?"

He turned towards her and said, "my father."

"Oh, what happened? Why would your mother have to run away from him?"

Dace responded with, "he use to beat her and occasionally beat me. He took his frustrations out on us periodically. Most of the time on my mother."

Nina stared at Dace completely in shock. He continued to say,

"She would buy me all these nice things and take me places to distract me. It didn't work though. I saw everything and heard everything. I never understood how a man who claimed to love my mother could beat her like that." He dropped his head in the palms of his hands.

Completely lost and bewildered, Nina stated, "let's take a walk."

They both got out the car and started to walk on the beach. The sun started to set. Holding his hand, Nina said, "look at that. It's so beautiful."

He nodded in agreement. Sensing something was wrong she began to ask him, "if you could change anything about yourself, what would it be?"

Dace took a deep breath and responded with, "my life choices. A lot of them were done out of anger. The end result was always bad. I mean, I'm not perfect, far from it but I definitely would change my actions if I could."

Nina stared at her feet getting lost into the sand on the beach then said, "your past doesn't define the man you are today. Just looking at you I wouldn't have known you had demons."

Dace looked her in her eyes and said, "my demons are dark and dangerous. You have no idea."

"Help me understand it Dace." Nina said curiously.

He kissed her lips and said, "maybe on a different day. We gotta head back to the city. I have a meeting tonight."

Looking confused Nina said, "for your restaurant?"

He looked down at his watch and responded with, "yeah something like that. It's a little business and some other things."

Nina didn't push the issue to continue to interrogate him so she just led the way to his jeep. She knew something was suspect about his responses. She knew if she kept digging he'd shut down. The best thing for her to do was let everything happen the way it should.

Dace drove them back to the city and parked at his condominium. He looked at Nina and said, "move in with me."

Taken back she said, "wait what!?"

"Yes Nina. Move in with me. Give me a reason to stay at home. I wanna wake up to you every morning and sleep with you every night. Be my comfort. My peace of mind. I feel I could have that with you."

He's bat shit crazy.

Nina stated in a concerned tone, "I just moved here. You've only been with me for a day and a half. We don't know each other like that."

Dace felt himself getting angry. He took a deep breath and said, "I just have a feeling we are meant for each other. Your energy is off the charts. It balances mine. When you know you know. Tell me I'm wrong."

Nina looked out the window to her car. Then responded with, "how about we go on a few more dates before we decide something so drastic like that. I haven't even started at my job yet, I have a lease at an apartment. I can't just break it."

He balled his fist up and quickly looked away from her. He let his window down to cool off. He quickly said to himself,

It's happening again.

"Look Nina. I know this can be special. But if more dates are what you need to realize it, fine." He felt defeated.

Nina nodded in agreeance.

"Well I know you have to get to your meeting. So I'll go back to my apartment." She started to get out his jeep and he accompanied her.

They walked to her car and he responded with, "until next time Nina." He kissed her on her forehead and gave her a hug.

"I'll let you know when I make it home." Nina said hoping to get a positive response.

"Okay." He stood in the parking lot until she pulled off. He proceeded to get in his jeep, but realized for this trip, he'd need to take his low key car. He grabbed the keys out the glove compartment and locked the doors. He went to his garage, opened it up, then unlocked his matte black BMW.

Showtime baby.

He drove to his warehouse where he keeps all his prized possessions. The only place that's off the grid. No signal for phone calls and is pitch black. At night, you need flashlights to maneuver through the warehouse.

He flicked his flashlight twice to signal Chubbs to come over to where he was. Within a few minutes, Dace heard heavy breathing.

"Yo D what's up?"

"I need a favor bro. I'm cashing in."

"Anything Dace."

Dace nodded in the darkness and responded with, "Barken is out, the body's gone, but his wife is still here. I need you to make that shit go away."

Chubbs eyes got big then stated, "Damn what the fuck did she do?"

"She knew he had ties with me. She knows he's missing so she's thinking about going to the cops to file a report. The cops caught my jeep on a camera. It didn't show my plates but with me being high profile they came to me. You need to get a jeep exactly like mine, register it to some random ass person, and put evidence in there from the crime scene after you take his bitch out. I need the heat off of me. I'm not going back to jail."

Chubbs nodded then said, "sayless."

Dace nodded then responded with, "text me when it's done."

They dabbed then left the warehouse.

Dace drove back to his condo with a peace of mind. He knew if he got caught up again, he'd be going to jail for life. Murder just don't go away especially for a black man in America. As he sat in his garage he felt his phone vibrate. He picked his phone up and saw a text from Nina.

I'm home. Thank you for the lovely day. It was definitely needed.

He responded with,

That's good. I'm glad you enjoyed your time. I'm looking forward to our next date.

He got out of his car then headed into his condo. Before he put the keys in the door. He felt his phone vibrate again. It was Khalil.

That nigga got locked up.

What the fuck!?

I need some furniture in here.

Nina paced back and forth while eating a slice of cold pizza. It wasn't her ideal breakfast, but it hit the spot.

What am I doing? I should've just moved in with the guy. I don't have shit here anyway.

It seemed like Sunday came so quick for her. She barely slept thinking about how her first day would go at her job tomorrow. She just hoped she wasn't pushing papers.

She wanted to get out there and make a difference. She checked her emails on her phone and saw an important email from her law firm.

New Case Alert   **Sunday, July 2nd**

From: **JakeStoaks@smlawfirm.net**

To: **Nina_Smith@jetzson.com**

Hello Miss Nina,

I hope your weekend is going well. Monday will be a busy day. I will have you go to Icington Correctional Facility to talk to our new client. His name is Gregory "Chubbs" Kent. He was arrested for speeding and this is his third strike as well. Attached is the address.

The Icington Correctional Facility knows you are coming. Bring your license and work ID as well. Be there by 9:00 am. Afterwards you will come back after getting to know your client and we will talk about best solutions to your case. If you have any questions, don't hesitate to call me at 217-MSL-FIRM.

Best wishes,

Jack Stoaks,

Marmen & Stoaks Law Firm

She quickly responded then looked in her suitcase for something to wear. She knew she had to look professional. There was no way she was going to walk into the correctional facility and not look like a lawyer. She saw her navy blue suit Joan bought her as a congratulations gift.

She always knew exactly what I needed.

She took her black pumps out and accompanied it with her navy blue snakeskin briefcase.

Pearls will do.

After getting her outfit in order, she decided to set up her next date with Dace. She knew she liked how things were going but knew there was a lot she needed to learn about him before moving in. Before she could pick up her phone she heard it vibrate.

Dace:

Hey. What do you have a taste for? I'll send it.

She smiled then replied with:

Italian. Surprise me.

He then responded with:

Address miss.

She paused. Took a deep breath then said:

379 E. Flagstin Ave

Dace:

Thank you, I'll order your food right away. Enjoy.

Nina:

Thank you so much. I must've lost track of time. I was so busy with getting everything set up for my first day that I didn't realize it was dinner time.

```
Dace:

No problem. That's why I'm here. To
help you.
```

After reading his response she decided to hop in the shower. She was interrupted with her doorbell ringing just shortly after.

Shit that's the food.

She hurried out the shower, dried off then wrapped herself in a towel. She opened the door and saw a delivery guy holding two bags of food.

"Hello, are you Nina?"

She looked down at his name tag and responded with, "Yes Trent. Thank you so much for the delivery. Here's a tip."

He shook his head no then stated, "that won't be necessary, Dace covered it already."

She then looked down at the bags and saw it was from Sherry's Brewery. She began to chuckle then took the bags. Trent then said, "enjoy mam."

She closed her door, then texted Dace. She felt he needed to know when the food arrived.

Hey. My food is here. Thanks again.

Dace:

Enjoy beautiful.

He ordered three meat lasagna, accompanied with Chicken Parmesan. There was a side of breadsticks, a garlic butter dipping sauce, a bottle of red wine, and two desserts: cannolis and tiramisu pie. She loved food. Her eyes lit up as the aroma of her delivery filled her nostrils.

She grabbed her fork and began to enjoy her full spread of Italian inspired foods. They were so delicious that a single tear fell from her eye.

Jesus take the wheel!

She waved her hands from side to side and started to dance. As she danced without music, her mind was set free. No worries, no stress, just pure happiness.

She caused herself to stop in place after burping. She walked over to her phone as saw that time had won today. It was a little after 10 pm and she knew that morning would come quick. She threw away all her empty containers then laid down. She blew up her air mattress then laid on her olive green silk pillowcase. She set her alarm on her phone then drifted off into dreamland.

Dace's phone began to ring. He took a deep breath because he knew who it was.

"You have a collect call from Chubbs. An inmate at Icington Correctional Facility. Do you accept the charges?"

He rolled his eyes then responded with, "yeah."

When the call connected, he began to hear heavy breathing.

"Yo nigga." Dace started the conversation. He knew he'd have to keep the conversation short and sweet. He's been through this so he knew the cops were listening in.

"Aye. I was going 7 miles above the speed limit, mufuckas on bullshit with me man." Chubbs responded tensely.

"Aw damn man. When are they letting you go?"

Dace wanted the job to get done. He needed Barken's wife to be killed. Chubbs was his fallback plan. Dace hadn't had to clean up any messes in a long time because a lot of people in his circle didn't test him. They all knew of him as a killer second but business man first. He really didn't want to get his hands dirty but at this point, he didn't have a choice.

Chubbs took a deep breath then said, "man, I don't know. It's my third strike. They don't play about that shit. I'm meeting with a lawyer in about an hour.

"Iight nigga. Let me know what's good afterwards." Dace thought about taking the wife out himself. He knew she'd remember his face so the odds of her snitching was high. At least if he sent Chubbs, she wouldn't have known him. He was in a tough position.

"Iight one."

Dace hung up the phone then yelled, "FUCK!"

He threw his glass of orange juice at the wall. The glass shattered immediately. He stood in one spot, staring at the wall drip of the drink. He shook his head then proceeded to grab a towel to clean up the mess.

That nigga betta keep it kosher with that fuckin lawyer.

"ID please."

Nina took both ids out and handed them to the officer.

"Here you go Officer Rhodes."

He began to type her information into the system then proceeded to give her instructions on going through the metal detector.

"You will receive your identification back after you checkout." He handed her a visitor's pass to stick on her blazer.

Nina nodded in agreeance, put the sticker on, then calmly walked through the metal detector.

"Right this way mam." An officer named Tiltin guided her to the visitation room then shut the door. "Inmate 8466 will be in shortly."

She looked around and saw just a metal table, two chairs, concrete walls, and a few windows. The lights were flickering on and off and it made her feel uneasy. Before being able to take a deep breath, she heard the door open.

"Sit down inmate."

Chubbs stared at the officer, then sat across from Nina. Being optimistic, Nina greeted him.

"Hello Gregory. I'm here from Marmen & Stoaks Law Firm. I'm Nina. It looks like you were arrested for speeding." She fondled through his file as he breathed heavily.

"Yea. Bullshit. They just wanted a reason to put me back here." He looked down at the cuffs on his wrists.

"Well, is there anything I need to know to further help your case?" Nina said hopefully.

"I don't talk to lawyers. I'm a go with the flow type of nigga." Looking puzzled, Nina asked, "well this is your third strike right?"

He responded with, "yea something like that."

"Okay Gregory, I can't help you if you don't give me straight answers." Nina said sounding convincing.

"Aye how about you talk to the dumb ass cop that pulled me over. 7 miles over the speed limit? Come on bro."

She sensed him getting irritated so she cut the conversation short.

"Okay. I will go to the precinct after I speak to my boss. I'm sure we'll be able to get you out of here. Just stay positive. You will hear from me soon." Nina extended her hand out to shake Chubbs hand but the officer yelled out, "NO PHYSICAL CONTACT!"

She immediately grabbed her items and walked out the door.

"Let's go inmate."

Chubbs stood up, shook his head then walked back to his cell.

It's over for me.

XII

Damn man.

Chubbs stared at his prison cell walls as the door closed. He stood up then began to pace back and forth. His stomach growled from not eating the slop of refried beans and cornbread they gave him earlier.

He knew Kimmy wasn't going to forgive him for messing up again. She had been his rock through a lot of his hard times.

They met after he got out of jail the first time. It happened after he graduated from high school. A lost graduate who didn't know what he wanted to be in life.

His mom passed away when he was 5 and his dad was a drug kingpin who was taken out when Chubbs was a preteen in jail while serving his life sentence. Needless to say, he didn't have any living biological parents. Just a kid who got lost in the system.

He had to grow up quickly. He went from foster home to foster home. He knew he had to hustle to get money. He would shoplift and sell the items he stole to classmates. Throughout his elementary and high school years, he spent the money he had on clothes, shoes, and food.

He ate so much that he became overweight. He started to use his weight to his advantage and began to scare people into giving him whatever he wanted. He'd beat up people if they said no and didn't think twice about it.

He ended up getting his first charge fresh out of high school. Caught shoplifting at the mall. He did his time then noticed that jail had everything he didn't have in the outside world. A brotherhood, hot meals, and his own bed. Throughout his foster days, a lot of the places he stayed at had two or three kids to one bed. He hated having to share anything.

After doing his time, he left the correctional facility and went to the local gas station for something to drink. He walked in the door to get a raspberry lemonade. He went up to the register and pulled a few bucks out his pocket. As he looked up, he saw a light skin freckled woman behind the counter. Her hair was dark brown and naturally curly. She wore a dark blue polo that had Icington gas and grocery stitched on the right side of it and some jeans.

Her name tag read Kimmy.

"$2.98." she said as she locked eyes with Chubbs.

138

He stared at her and completely lost his train of thought.

"Excuse me sir." Kimmy said as he was knocked back into reality.

"Aw shit, my bad." He handed her 3 dollars.

She chuckled and said, "it's okay." She handed him his change and then said, "have a nice day."

As he walked out the store, he looked down at his receipt. He saw she wrote her number on it.

Before getting arrested, he had a one bedroom apartment. Living with foster parents had it perks because he was able to save his money and plan for his future moves. He waved down a cab then went back to his apartment. He saw his phone was sitting on the counter.

Damn man, so many missed calls. Missed opportunities.

He only served a year but he knew he had to get back in the business. He started making phone calls to let people know he was out of jail. He went back to what he knew best, shoplifting. This time he wanted to go about it differently. He bought a gun. He wanted people to know he was about his money. So cash out or die. Plain and simple. But luckily, he never had to drop a body.

After a while, he was comfortable enough to start inviting Kimmy over. They had gone on multiple dates, he spent the night over at her place, she cooked for him all the time, the whole nine. They made things official after 4 months of talking. As things started to go good, he felt he needed to let her know what he does for a living. She didn't support it at all. She knew what could eventually happen to him. He assured her that he was on top of it.

He ended up getting arrested again after getting pulled over for a broken taillight. They had suspicions that he may have had something else in his car so they searched it. They found his gun and immediately arrested him. Knowing he let Kimmy down, he promised her, "I'm gonna change baby. Please don't leave me. I don't know what I'd do without you by my side. I don't have anybody else."

"Prove it." Kimmy hung up the phone.

After getting released, he moved in with Kimmy. He got a good job working for an electronics company. He eventually proposed to Kimmy and they got married.

Since he didn't have any family, he didn't have anybody to invite to the wedding. A month later, he took the garbage out to the alleyway from their apartment. He was confronted by a guy who he had robbed.

"Aye fat fuck! You remember me!?"

Chubbs turned around and was confronted by a guy wearing a hoodie with loose fitting jeans. He was pointing a gun at him. Chubbs felt his pockets then immediately remembered he didn't have his gun anymore.

Shit.

He tried to reason with the guy. "Look man. I've changed, I have a wife and she's pregnant." Chubbs held his hands up hoping the guy would have put the gun down.

The angry man proceeded to say, "I don't give a fuck!!! Where's my car? Huh? Where's my money you stole nigga?"

Chubbs stood there in a trance. He didn't know how to answer because he clearly didn't have those items anymore. He had stop stealing from people. He was just trying to get his life on the right track.

"L—Look man." Chubbs stuttered as he saw Dace run up behind the guy. Dace knocked the guy clean out with a glass bottle. He then punched the man continuously until all he saw was blood rushing from his face. Dace and Chubbs started to hear sirens.

"Run nigga!!" Dace said as he continued to beat the guy up.

Chubbs ran back up to his apartment and held Kimmy. Tears ran down his face because he knew at some point his life would always be about breaking the law. Karma was coming back to bite him and knew he had to get ahead of it.

He started to look around town for Dace but it seemed like he had disappeared. He eventually found out he had got locked up for 5 years. After he got out, Chubbs saw him at the gas station after dropping off Kimmy's lunch.

"Hey nigga, what's good?" Chubbs dabbed Dace.

Dace responded with, "nothing much. Just got out."

"Well damn, welcome home." Chubbs nodded then continued to thank him. "Aye man, you don't know how much I'm grateful for what you did back then. Whatever favor you need, no matter what it is, I got you nigga."

"How about you work for me for the time being. You gotta work off that 5 year stent I did for your ass. I'm sure I can pay you more than whatever you're making now anyway. Plus, I know I'll need to cash in on your favor at some point. I just can't think of what yet." Dace knew exactly what he wanted to do with him.

Dace had a few people he had to pay a visit to. He protected the majority of the city from evictions. After he gave them loans, they had to pay him in return for his services. But sometimes, people wouldn't pay on time or not pay what they were suppose to. Dace would either give them another chance or kill them.

He needed another person in his circle to get rid of the evidence. He felt as if Chubbs could be taught the proper way to make things disappear. He knew he was a shoplifter by heart because he only got caught once. He was good at hiding things.

Chubbs had another baby on the way and knew his job wouldn't give him more hours to accommodate his new expenses. He agreed to work for Dace. He lied to Kimmy about where the stacks of money were coming from. She knew something wasn't right, but she was taken care of and so were their kids.

She had given up a long time ago with trying to keep him on the straight and narrow. She just wanted him to come home to her and be the family man after he did his dirt.

Chubbs knew he'd get caught up eventually. He started to go back to carrying guns around. His job for Dace consisted of constantly going into places cleaning up behind a crime scene.

After a while, it became routine for him. He'd get the phone call from Dace then go about his business. He always made sure to get rid of camera feeds from their businesses, blood, weapons, and bodies.

After finding out about Dace's jeep getting got caught on a traffic camera, he knew he had to find another jeep quick. He had never killed a person. He was always the one there to clean it up afterwards. He felt sick to his stomach knowing Dace finally said what he wanted his favor to be.

After leaving his meeting with Dace, he became completely distracted by his own thoughts. He began to speed. He looked in his rear view mirror and saw flashing blue lights.

FUCK!

He was snapped back into reality when he heard the officers say, "lights out."

As the whole jail went into complete darkness, tears fell from his eyes.

I gotta get out of here.

XIII

Nina walked into the law firm feeling defeated. She felt like nothing got accomplished when she met with her client. He seemed very uneasy and irritated which in turn made her feel uncomfortable. She joined Marmen & Stoaks because she knew she'd get challenging cases. Nina always wanted to help people but in her own way.

"Good Morning Miss. Smith." Jenny greeted her at the front desk.

"Hey Jenny, good morning." Nina showed her ID, then proceeded to go to Mr. Stoaks office.

She knocked and he looked up from signing paperwork. "Hello, please come in." He smiled as she walked towards the chair in front of his desk.

"So how was your visit with Mr. Kent?" Stoaks asked optimistically.

Looking defeated Nina responded with, "well his answers were very vague. He honestly didn't say much sir."

"And he's aware of this being his third strike right?" Mr. Stoaks asked for confirmation.

"Yes Sir." Nina nodded.

He took a deep breath then stated, "okay I need you to go down to the precinct. See what they're looking to charge him with and how much time they are going to ask for. It's a very minor charge but you never know with these people. With it being his third strike, they might be looking to put him away for a while. Try to fight for our client and don't leave unless there's a reasonable resolution. They have a local district attorney on site there named Emmanuel Cho. They'll most likely send you to his office after speaking with them."

149

"Okay Sir. Thank you." She commended him as she wrote down notes.

"Call me when you leave." As he said that his phone started to ring. She knew that was her cue to walk out his office and head to the Icington Police Department.

She parked then walked in and was greeted by an officer running the front desk.

"Can I help you mam?" The officer asked curiously.

"Oh yes, I'm Nina Smith from Marmen & Stoaks law firm. I'm here to talk about my client Gregory Kent. I'm representing him in his speeding case. I need to talk to the person who's in charge." Nina said professionally.

The police officer nodded then responded, "okay, one moment."

The officer began typing on his computer. He typed Gregory's name in and immediately saw more than just a speeding charge on his record. He grabbed the phone then said, "Yes sir. A representative from Marmen & Stoaks Law firm is here. She's here about Gregory Kent."

The officer nodded then hung up the phone. He then looked at Nina and said, "Mr. Cho will be right with you."

She waited at the front desk for about 20 minutes before being greeted by the district attorney.

He stood in front of her and said, "sorry for my tardiness, I'm DA Emmanuel Cho." He extended his hand out to Nina. She politely shook his hand then responded with, "nice to meet you Sir."

"Follow me Miss." He started to walk towards his office. He sat down then proceeded to say, "so what brings you here?"

Taken back Nina stated, "I'm here on behalf of my client Gregory Kent. He was arrested yesterday because he was speeding 7 miles over the speed limit. My client and I feel that the rational for this charge is unreasonable. Everybody speeds at some point. He should've been given a warning but because he's been arrested before, he was taken in. He's not a repeated reckless driver."

Emmanuel nodded then looked at his watch.

Nina continued to plead her case by saying, "He's never been arrested for it before so what are you willing to do for him? Because if we take this court, I will request records for all offenders that have gotten a slap on the wrist for speeding and I will be asking for a payout from your office for my client's pain and suffering and request all charges be dropped."

He chuckled then said, "we were never gonna charge him with speeding mam. We needed him in custody for a different matter."

Sounding confused Nina asked, "what different matter sir?"

He went to his file cabinet then took out a manila envelope. He reached in it and placed photos on his desk. "We have reason to believe he's an accomplice to a murder."

Nina's eyes got big then responded with, "wait what!? Murder?"

Emmanuel then continued to explain, "there were gunshots heard coming from Barken's laundromat a few days ago. The owner has yet to turn up and we have a witness that heard the conversation prior to shots being fired and shortly after. The cameras were wiped clean, no blood, no body as well. Our witness saw Gregory's face in that laundromat after everything went down. After showing our witness pictures of mugshots, it was in fact confirmed he was there."

Emmanuel then showed her a picture of him driving out from behind the laundromat.

Nina shook her head then stated, "that could be anybody in that vehicle Cho. There's no way you can charge him with this. This is he say she say."

"Oh, the person was hiding inside the bathroom of the laundromat mat. The person peaked out when some heavy footed person was walking around and saw his face. Then the witness didn't come out until the police came. There aren't too many heavy footed people in this town Nina. Your client is guilty.

"But I'll make it easy for you. If he's willing to give up the shooter and agrees to be a criminal informant to nail that son of a bitch who actually killed Barken, we'll let him go. If not, he'll be charged with being an accomplice. He'll never see his wife and kids again."

He's married? Jesus.

Nina nodded then said, "Wow. I will talk to Mr. Stoaks then come up with the best solution. We'll be in touch."

"If I were you, I'd hurry Miss Smith. The offer expires in 24 hours." Emmanuel stood up and opened his door for her to walk out.

"Nice meeting you Mr. Cho." Nina walked out his office mind blown. There was no way her client could've did those things. She always wanted to see the good in people even when the end result was the complete opposite. She got in her car then proceeded to call her boss.

"Hello, Mr. Stoaks speaking."

"Hey it's Nina, we have a problem."

XIV

"So do you want me to present this plea deal to him?"

Mr. Stoaks took a deep breath then proceeded to say, "well we don't have a choice. Either he wants to rot behind bars or get back to his family. His decision is bigger then just himself."

Nina nodded in agreeance. "I'll head back there now."

"Okay Nina, it's almost 1 pm, visiting hours are over at 3." He hung up the phone hoping she'd be able to get there in time.

Her phone vibrated. It was Dace.

Hey. I hope your day is going well.

She saw his message then quickly drove to the jail. Her day was pretty busy. She went from dealing with a speeding case to a possible accomplice to a murder case. One hell of a difference.

She felt nervous because she didn't know if Gregory would deny being there. She didn't know how to react to him possibly lying. She knew that it was him in the picture that was shown but wasn't going to incriminate her client.

Okay Nina let's do this.

She went through the check in process then waited for Chubbs to come to the visitation room.

"Sit down inmate."

"I'm guessing you got some news for me." Chubbs said feeling optimistic. He needed some good news. Kimmy hadn't been answering her phone. He knew he had messed up.

She had already threatened to take the kids and leave Icington before he got arrested after they fought over him staying out too late working. This could've been the straw that broke the camel's back.

"Okay. We need to talk. I need you to be completely honest." Nina said sternly.

What the fuck is she talking about? All I did was speed.

She went in her briefcase and took out the pictures she was shown at the precinct. "Is that you Gregory?"

His eyes got extremely big then responded with, "fuck no I'm being set up!"

She rolled her eyes. She was annoyed at the fact that he blatantly lied to her face. But she knew she was dealing with a criminal. All her life she gave people the benefit of the doubt. She hated that about herself. She knew she had to toughen up to get her point across.

159

She yelled, "Listen dumb ass! Don't lie to me!"

Completely in shock, he said "look calm down."

"No! You're running out of time here. The DA has a witness that saw you at the scene. Somebody was shot at that laundromat and is missing. They're assuming the person is dead. They're accusing you of cleaning up the scene. Is anything I'm saying true!?"

He stared at her in shock. He was speechless. He never once dropped the ball when it came to crime scenes until now. His hands were tied. He didn't know how to respond.

"Answer me Gregory!!"

"Okay, okay. Yes I was there but I didn't kill any—"

Before he could finish his statement, she cut him off.

"Where's the body Gregory?"

He put his head down. "I can't tell you all of that."

"So he's dead?" Nina felt tears forming in her eyes.

Chubbs took a deep breath and said, "yes. All I did was get rid of the evidence. It's…..my job to do that."

Nina shook her head then took a deep breath. "We have to get ahead of this. The DA knows you had something to do with it. The only way this can go away is if you become a criminal informant."

He stood up and said, "fuck that!! I ain't no snitch!!"

She stood up and yelled, "You have a wife and kids to think about!"

He stood there shocked. He kept his personal life as private as possible. Clearly the cops had been watching him. He didn't want anybody to know he had a family just in case things with south with Dace. He knew family members were the first to go if the person Dace looked for was nowhere to be found. He was cold blooded when it came to sending messages.

161

"Listen. I don't need everybody knowing about my family. I'm trying to protect them." Chubbs pleaded.

"Sit back down." Nina said calmly.He listened.

"Look, the only way they're willing to drop the charges is if you work for them. They want to get the person who killed Barken."

Chubbs shook his head and he closed his eyes. He never thought he'd be in this predicament. He knew eventually Dace would find out he was a nark if he agreed to working with the cops. If that happened, he would get killed eventually. He wasn't willing to lose his life but he knew living behind bars while his kids grew up without him wasn't an option either.

"Gregory I need an answer."

Fuck it. I owe it to my family.

"I'll do it."

"I need to see you Nina." Dace begged. It had been a little over a week since he saw Nina.

She had been so caught up with getting Chubbs released, she forgot to contact Dace. She wasn't the type that wanted to let her job consume her but for the sake of Chubbs wife and kids, she had to make sure her client had the best chance of seeing them again.

"I'm so sorry, work has just been crazy. I'll see you soon. I promise." Nina tried to sound convincing but she honestly didn't know when she'd see him again. After finalizing the plea deal with Gregory and the District Attorney, Chubbs was successfully able to be released and start working as a criminal informant.

Nina's boss was impressed with her and immediately started giving her more clients. A lot of them were minor, but she wanted to prove she could be the best lawyer.

"Listen, let's go out Saturday." He said, as he started to clean his metal bat off. He had a busy week as well. Barken's wife ended up coming to his condominium and confronted him about her husband. Things got physical and he ended up beating her with his bat after he knocked her out. He had to get rid of the body quick so he didn't have time to clean up his apartment.

Since Chubbs was MIA, Dace had to pick up where he left off. Khalil knew of everything but stayed out of it. He knew if Dace needed him, he'd get in touch with him.

"Okay yes let's do that." Nina smiled as she put all her files away in her dresser. Although she was busy, she was able to pay for some furniture. Her place wasn't as big as Dace's but she had the essentials that made her place feel like home.

"How about I come over tonight." Dace needed to take his mind off his recent activities.

"Ohh um tonight isn't a good time. I'm still getting paper work together." He didn't know she was a lawyer and frankly she felt it wasn't his business. She felt if he knew, he'd look at her differently. All her life people judged her for having surgeons as parents.

"Why do I feel like you're ignoring me?" He asked irritatingly.

"Oh no it's not that. I just have a lot of stuff I need to have ready by next week."

"Fine Nina." He hung up the phone.

Completely in shock, she stared at her phone.

He's very clingy.

A part of her felt like she needed to see him but the other part of her felt like she needed to take a step back from Dace.

He didn't understand that she wanted to succeed at her job. All he cared about was seeing her. Everyday he attempted to text or call her. When he couldn't get her to answer, he'd leave notes on her car at her apartment building. She thought it was cute yet creepy. Little did she know it was only adding fuel to the fire.

I could use a night off.

"What the fuck could she possibly be doing!?" He said as he started cleaning up the dried up blood on the floor.

Dace let his anger get the best of him as he envisioned his last kill. Blood spatter was everywhere. He thought about moving, but he knew he'd attract too much attention if he did that.

He paced back at forth thinking about how he hadn't heard from Chubbs since the first phone call he had. He knew he was still locked up but he needed him out. The grunt work wasn't his place.

That's what he paid Chubbs for. Annoyed, he started pushing his mop back and forth. A few minutes after that, he heard a knock at his door.

Fuck.

His clothes was dirty from cleaning and he wasn't done yet. He still had to clean the walls. He had beat her head in to the point that her face was completely flat. Blood spattered everywhere. The knock got louder.

"Hold on DAMN!" He wasn't expecting company. So he didn't know who it was. He quickly took his shirt off then went to look through the peephole. "Aw nah. It can't be."

Taken back, he unlocked his door and saw Chubbs standing in front of him.

"Yoooooo!" Chubbs went in for a hug.

Completely surprised, Dace said to him, "what the fuck are you doing here nigga? I thought you was still locked up."

"They knew that speeding shit was bullshit. They let me out."

"Well welcome home nigga." Dace dabbed him after giving him a hug. He felt something on his back but ignored it. "You wanna come in?"

Chubbs scanned the room. He knew something was wrong. Something bad had happened there. He saw blood on the walls, and a bloody mop.

"Where's your shirt nigga?" Chubbs walked in the door, continuing to look around. "Is that blood!?"

Dace began to laugh, "my shirt dirty nigga. Why are you asking so many questions?"

Feeling a little uneasy, Chubbs responded with, "my bad man, I just see red shit on your mop and red shit on the wall over there."

"And? Why do you wanna know what happened here?" Dace asked irritatingly.

"Whoa chill, it just looks kinda weird in here. The vibes are off." Chubbs proceeded to sit down on the couch.

"Nah it's all good. Had to take care of some business. Shit got outta hand." Dace stated as he began to wipe the wall off.

"Aye what happened to Barken's wife?"

The cops noticed she went missing after trying to contact her on multiple occasions. They gave Chubbs strict instructions to find out what happened.

"Nigga it was handled." Dace started rinsing off the bloody towel.

"What do you mean?" Chubbs asked curiously.

"She's no longer a problem." Dace said as he finished cleaning his mop off.

"What happened, where is she? Where's the body?"

Dace knew something was up. Chubbs never asked those type of questions before. "Why?"

Chubbs held his head down then responded with, "look man I just wanna know."

"Uh huh." Dace walked in his room and went in his closet. He took his gun out.

Fuckin nark.

"Come on man you can trust me. Just tell me what happened." Chubbs walked over to his fridge and took a beer out.

"Nah." Dace stood in the kitchen and pointed his gun at him.

"What the fuck are you doing Dace!?" Chubbs dropped the beer and stood there with his hands up.

"You tell me nigga." Dace stood completely still and stared at Chubbs like he was taking his soul.

He looked at his chest then back at his face. Chubbs knew he was screwed.

"Look man. I had t—"

Before he could finish his statement, Dace shot him in between his eyebrows. As his body dropped to the floor, Dace walked up to him. He emptied his clip on him causing blood to splatter on his face and shirt.

Fuck. Now I gotta clean up again.

Before he could change, he heard a knock at the door again. He knew the cops weren't too far away but he knew they couldn't have got to him that fast. He walked to the door completely drenched in blood. Full of adrenaline, he opened the door.

"Nina."

She took a step back when she saw blood dripping from his face and a gun in his hand.

XVI

"W—What happened here!??" Nina continued to back up.

He knew he had to explain everything to her. "Please come in. I don't have much time."

"I'm okay." Nina started to walk towards the elevators.

"God dammit!! Get over here!!" He ran towards her grabbing her arm and pulled her into his condo. "I need your help." Dace threw a towel towards her.

Nina stared at the floor. "Oh my God! What did you do to Gregory!?"

He turned to her and said, "how do you know him!?"

"He was my client! Come on we have to get him to a hospital!"

Dace then stated, "client?"

She turned towards him then put two and two together. Clearly he was the one that killed Barken. She felt so stupid for not putting together the facts. She thought back to the day he left her at his condo and came back with a completely different shirt on.

Tears filled her eyes. She knew he said he had dark demons but killing people was the last thing she thought he was talking about.

"I can't believe this! I have to go!" As she tried to run for the door, he immediately stood in front of it.

"Nah you're gonna help me clean this shit up. I gotta leave before the cops find me." Dace grabbed her arm and directed her towards the body.

"I'm not helping you! You're bat shit crazy!" She snatched her arm back then attempted to push him out the way. When she was unsuccessful, she punched him in the face.

"Ahhh you fuckin BITCH!!" Dace held his eye as blood started to pour out of it. One of her rings hit him in his eye socket.

She ran out the door and managed to escape his condominium. She ran for her life, rain flowing and cops sirens soaring through her ears. She knew he wasn't too far behind her.

She ran to Sherry's Brewery but nobody wanted to help her. They saw her through the glass as she banged on the windows.

She felt defeated as she continued to run while yelling, "HELLLPPPP!!!!"

She ended up going through alleys and side streets. She felt like she lost him. She took a deep breath and reminisced on her first days in Incington. She couldn't understand how the man she met her first day here was a cold blooded killer.

"That was my eye Bitch!" He stood right in front of her with his hand wrapped around her neck. Her airway was starting to close. Her face began to look lifeless and her lips began to turn blue. She used what little energy she had to say, "why?"

Before she could get an answer, she dropped to the ground.

Dace stared at her lifeless body. He had no emotion for what he had done. Throughout his life, he felt every kill he made was justified. He thought about how things could've been different if she had just helped.

As he began to walk out the alley he was stopped by a barricade of cops blocking him from both ends.

179

"FREEZE MOTHERFUCKER!! PUT YOUR HANDS WHERE WE CAN SEE THEM!"

Dace dropped his head.

"Put your fuckin hands up!!"

Guns pointed from every direction, he looked around and he smiled.

This is gonna be fun.

www.ingramcontent.com/pod-product-compliance
Lightning Source LLC
Chambersburg PA
CBHW060944180626
46817CB00004B/1705